Dear Connor

Some stories from India
and Bangladesh, to go
with your love of
geography

Love from Aunt Carol

Robi Dobi

Robi Dobi

THE MARVELOUS ADVENTURES OF
AN INDIAN ELEPHANT

MADHUR JAFFREY

Illustrated by Amanda Hall

DIAL BOOKS FOR YOUNG READERS
NEW YORK

For Robi
my precious

First published in the United States in 1997 by
DIAL BOOKS FOR YOUNG READERS
A Division of Penguin Books USA Inc.
375 Hudson Street
New York, New York 10014

Published in Great Britain 1996
by Pavilion Books Limited
Text copyright © 1996 by Madhur Jaffrey
Illustrations copyright © 1996 by Amanda Hall
All rights reserved
Printed in Hong Kong
First Edition
1 3 5 7 9 10 8 6 4 2

Library of Congress Cataloging in Publication Data
Jaffrey, Madhur.
Robi Dobi: the marvelous adventures of an Indian elephant/by Madhur Jaffrey;
illustrated by Amanda Hall.
p. cm.
Summary: An Indian elephant befriends a mouse, a butterfly, and a parrot,
and together they have many adventures.
ISBN 0-8037-2193-5
[1. Elephants—Fiction. 2. Animals—Fiction. 3. India—Fiction.]
I. Hall, Amanda, ill. II. Title.
PZ7.J15344Ro   1997   [Fic]—dc20   96-28977   CIP   AC

Contents

How This Story Started

My father was a busy man.

He got up early in the morning, had his first cup of tea sitting in an easy chair set out in the verandah or the garden, then had his bath, then his breakfast of two fried eggs and toast (he always ate the egg whites first and then the yolks, all in one bite), and then he left for the office.

The office was a mysterious place where my father did mysterious things. All I knew was that, as he was about to leave, my mother filled up his slim, silver cigarette case for the day and put as many rupees as he would need into his beautiful black leather wallet. And then my father stepped into his latest model car, English or American as his whim dictated, and off he went, smelling good and looking good.

He nearly always came back at the same time, just as the sun was getting low behind our western garden wall. Sometimes he played badminton or tennis on our lawns, but often he took my hand and we went for a walk in the garden. In the flower garden he told me about the roses that needed to be grafted and how one can eat the middle of a marigold. In the vegetable garden he explained how potatoes grow underground and how green beans grow on vines that need support.

Then we would come indoors. There was more tea and evening baths. After that my father had his single Scotch whisky with soda and listened to the news on the BBC radio. We always had dinner together: It could be quails that were cooked with cardamom, tiny new potatoes from our garden cooked with cumin seeds and green beans, also our own, cooked with ginger.

Soon it would be our bedtime. It was then that my father told us his stories. He never read stories to us. Perhaps, because we were all such good and constant readers (he called us bookworms), he felt we needed something else. My father just made up his stories.

They must have come to him easily. He had, after all, grown up in a storytelling family. It is the custom in our large community to tell stories at every religious celebration. Usually these are stories of the gods that are worshipped at specific festivals. The style of storytelling is, however, quite unique. Some of the myths that are retold are probably hundreds, if not thousands, of years old. But in my family they are retold as if they are happening today and are the experience of that particular family alone.

For example, if the story is being told to a child that has just been to America, a very traditional ancient Indian demon might be heard to mutter, "I will tear you apart and chew you up with all my ten mouths, unless of course, you can, within five minutes, provide me with a hundred hamburgers—with ketchup and onion." If the child hearing the story has a splinter in his thumb, then the storyteller might well make sure that the leading god also has a splinter in his thumb. If a Russian ballet troupe is visiting and we have just seen a performance, the dance troupe too is woven in. In other words, the particular art of storytelling in my family easily mixes ancient tradition with the very modern and personal. The language used in the storytelling is completely contemporary, full of onomatopoeic sounds.

My father told his stories in the same spirit, only his stories were entirely original. The story that I liked best was about an adventurous elephant who liked to help other creatures. The elephant always came across a small animal or bird or insect in trouble, heard its story, and then helped it overcome whatever its problem happened to be. This particular story could continue as long as my father liked, sometimes for weeks on end. It could be revived whenever we wished. My father could always create new stories with fresh characters. The only constant was the elephant.

Fifty-five years later, while I remembered that my father had told us stories about the adventures of a kindly elephant, I could not remember any of the stories themselves. What did stick in my head, very clearly, was the line, "and the elephant said, 'Come into my ear.'" (*"Hathi nay kaha, 'ajao maray kaan mai.'"*) You see, whenever the elephant found a little creature in trouble, he would first hear its story and then begin by offering it shelter in his big ear. "Come into my ear," he would say. The minute we children heard those words, we would all begin shaking with excitement. We knew that the adventure was off to a good start.

When I decided to write this book, I asked my sisters if they perhaps remembered some of the elephant tales. They did not. They only remembered the same single line that I did, "and the elephant said, 'Come into my ear.'" There was surely one story about a butterfly. What were the others?

I decided to do what my father had done—invent my stories. But in his spirit and in the spirit of my ancestors, using a main character that is now a part of our family history.

I could not recall what my father had named his elephant. I have called mine Robi Dobi. Robi is the nickname of our first grandson, Rohan. My father would have enjoyed the continuity—his great-grandson becoming part of his story. The major part of this book was written well before our second grandchild, Cassius, was born. Don't worry, little Cash, you will be woven into the story later. By me, or who knows, perhaps by your mother!

Madhur Jaffrey

ONE

A Narrow Escape

Tha thump.

Tha thump.

Tha thump. . . . Heavy feet landed gently on the wet leaves and twigs. It was raining hard. The monsoon winds were blowing the raindrops into swirling sheets, making the mighty trees of the forest sway and shake.

Then it began to thunder. C-r-aaa-ck. Lightning zigzagged across the dark sky.

Robi Dobi was on his way home to his family. He usually enjoyed the long walk through the forest to his home, a cave in a distant hill, but today was such a nasty day.

Robi Dobi decided to take a shortcut across the river. He took one step into the water. Oooops. The current was strong. Better be careful, he said to himself. Putting one foot firmly in front of the other, he managed to get to the middle of the river. It was here, above the din of the waters, that he heard a little squeaking sound.

"Help me, help me!"

The small squeaking sound was coming from somewhere along the river.

"Help me, please, please help me!"

Where on earth was that voice coming from? Robi Dobi turned this way and that. He could not see a thing.

"I'm here, I'm here. Just behind you. Save me, Mr. Elephant."

As Robi Dobi turned, there was a flash of lightning, and in the brightness he could see in front of him a little thing—a little, bright orange mouselike thing—clinging to a large teak leaf that floated in the churning water. The leaf bobbed up and down, and with it the little mouselike thing went under the water, then out of the water, then under the water, all the time crying miserably, "Help me, please save me." Robi Dobi was not sure what kind of creature it was. It certainly looked like a mouse, but its bright orange appearance made him wonder.

"I am coming," trumpeted Robi Dobi. "Now stay calm. I am going to stretch out my trunk to you. Climb onto it and hang on tight. Then I will put you in my ear. You will be safe there."

It was not so easy. Every time Robi Dobi stretched out his trunk, the leaf with the mouselike creature clinging to it floated farther away. Finally Robi very cleverly looped the end of his trunk and hooked the teak leaf. The shivering mouselike creature ran up his trunk.

"Achoo, achoo." He sneezed several times. "Oh, I am so cold, Mr. Elephant."

"Just climb inside my ear and snuggle up. You will find it very cozy and comfortable there," Robi reassured him. The little mouse crawled into Robi's ear.

Slowly and carefully Robi crossed the river. Once he was on the other side, he called out to the creature he was sheltering. "So how are you doing in there?"

"I-I a-am w-warming u-up n-n-now. You h-have cozy little nooks here, Mr. Elephant. I think I can finally relax and rest." The creature shivered for a while, but eventually he curled up and settled down for a snooze. By the time he woke again, it had stopped raining and the clouds had begun to clear.

Robi Dobi heard the mouselike creature moving in his ear so he called out to him, "Good morning to you. My name is Robi Dobi, but you can call me Robi. And what should I call you? I do not mean to be rude," Robi continued, "but what exactly are you? You look rather like a mouse, but you cannot possibly be because you are orange."

"Oh, I am a mouse all right. My name is Kabbi, Kabbi Wahabbi, and I come from the village of Trig-nig-wig-put-num."

"My, you have come a long way," Robi said.

"I-I know," said the mouse, and started to cry.

Robi could not bear to see anyone in pain. "Do you want me to take you back to Trig-nig-wig-put-num?" he offered.

"It is so complicated," Kabbi said. "You see, I left home because . . . it is such a long story."

"I have a little time to listen," Robi said.

Kabbi let out a big sigh. "Well, here is my story," he said.

TWO

Kabbi Wahabbi's Story

"I started out as just a plain brown mouse growing up in a family of eight. Six brothers and sisters, and my parents, of course. We used to eat and sleep in the rice fields. When the rice fields were flooded with water, we stayed in holes near the edges. We came out only to eat and play. There were always enough rice grains to keep us fed and happy. Nobody noticed us, as we blended in with the earth.

"Then one day, Slimy Kimey the snake-witch came to live in Trig-nig-wig-put-num. She was so bad that when she passed along a lane, all the houses and trees turned away from her. Her breath was bad, her smell was bad, and she always carried a long, slim can of—oh dear, oh dear—of horrible, smelly, permanent orange spray-paint." Kabbi's voice got even more high-pitched as he thought of the paint.

"You see, Slimy liked to eat mice. Whenever she saw a mouse from a distance, she shot a long, thin spray of paint at it, and then, once the mouse was painted bright orange, she could spot it wherever it went. It could hide in its hole for a while, but it had to come out sometime to search for rice grains to eat, and it was then that the wicked Slimy Kimey grabbed it and took it home to fatten up for her mouse pie."

"How awful for you, how terrible, how really terrible," Robi said, shaking his head and wiggling his ears.

"Please, Robi—do not shake your head and wiggle your ears. I am still feeling a little unwell."

"I am so sorry," said Robi. "I will try and keep my head still. Tell me, what happened next?"

"The worst, the worst," Kabbi squeaked. "My father gave us all a long lecture. He said that none of us was ever to leave our hole. He would go out to look for rice grains, and he would be very, very careful."

"And then?" Robi asked.

"We were so scared," Kabbi said. "At first no one went out. We stayed in our hole. Then when we got very hungry, Father said that he would go and find food. He told us not to worry. But he never came back. Then Mother said that it was her turn to go. She told us not to worry. She said that she would find Father as well as some rice grains, and that she would return as soon as possible. But she did not come back either.

"We were all so hungry. And worried. Then my eldest brother went to look for food, and then the next brother. Soon all my brothers and sisters had gone and I was the only one left. At first I cried a lot, but then I decided that the only thing to do was look for my family and try to find some food as well.

"I poked my head out of the hole and looked this way and that. I couldn't see any danger, so I crept out. There were a few rice grains lying just outside our hole. I started to eat them. Just then I felt a sharp sting and wetness. . . . I was drowning in sticky, orange wetness.

"I turned my head. There, laughing madly, was the wicked witch, Slimy Kimey, with her can of permanent orange paint. I started running, but the paint was so gluey, it was hard to move. My feet stuck to the ground.

"I finally managed to climb up a tree. But when the tree saw Slimy Kimey coming, it swayed away from her and shook me off.

"I kept trying to run. Slimy Kimey was catching up with me. I was out of breath. Slimy Kimey was almost on top of me. I squeaked for help, but no one wanted to come near Slimy Kimey. I felt a hand reach out and grab me. Slimy Kimey picked me up and brought me right up to her face. She really smelled bad. 'You will taste so good in my mouse pie,' she said, 'but first I have to fatten you up.'

"At that point I lunged out and bit her nose. She screamed and let go of me. I ran as fast as I could, but Slimy Kimey was just behind me.

"I came to a rushing river and jumped onto a large teak leaf that was floating on the water. The river was so rough that I did not know which was worse—being thrown around on the water or being chased by Slimy Kimey. I was whirling farther and farther from Slimy Kimey, which was good, but also farther and farther from Trig-nig-wig-put-num, which was not good.

"Just when I was sure that I was going to drown, I saw what I thought was a rock. But it was moving. It was you. That was when I yelled for help—and you know what happened next."

"I will take care of you, little mouse," Robi said. "First, we have to get the paint off. . . . "

"But this is permanent paint. It will never come off," Kabbi squeaked.

"I know somebody who can help," Robi declared. "You see that sky? You see how it is light blue in places, red in others? You see how there are purple patches and pink splashes and deep blue gashes? How do you think that happens?"

"I cannot see it too well from inside your ear," Kabbi replied.

"Well then, come out and take a stroll on my back. You will get a very good view. It has turned into a beautiful evening."

Kabbi came out and strolled on Robi's back. Then he sat down, leaning on one of Robi's bumps, and crossed his legs. "If I wasn't orange, if I wasn't so far from home, and if I wasn't worrying about my family, I would really enjoy this," he admitted.

"As I was saying," Robi went on, "why do you think the sky looks so beautiful?"

"I don't know. I never thought about it. Why does it?" Kabbi asked.

"It is all the work of Kamala-Saurus, The Great Painter in the Sky."

"The Great Painter in the Sky? Who is that?" Kabbi asked.

"She is very old," Robi said. "Ever since the beginning of the world, which was a long time ago, she has been painting the sky.

"Even before morning has started, she takes out all her brushes, making sure that they are clean and firm. She takes out all her pots of paints and arranges them neatly—indigo and ultramarine, cobalt blue and carmine red, crimson and sap green, yellow ochre and aqua.

"She busily mixes her paints and starts by painting the dawn—purplish blue and bluish black and pinkish red, with great bursts of gold. She has to hold the brushes in her mouth: You see, she has a very long neck and this way she can reach any part of the sky.

"As the day goes on, she paints the sky a light blue and fills it with light or dark clouds, according to the weather. She even paints in lightning when it is needed—beautiful zigzags of pure silver. Later, at night, she has to paint in a dark blue sky and, of course, all the millions of stars."

"A-mazing, a-mazing," squeaked Kabbi, "but I don't need anything painted. I need just the opposite. I need all this orange paint removed."

"I was just coming to that," Robi said. "Late every night Kamala-Saurus cleans off all her brushes. She has hundreds of cleaning waters. Some she gets from lakes in the highest of the Himalayan mountains, others she gets from special streams or rivers. Still others she gets from faraway seas. Only she knows where to find her special paints and all the waters that can wash them off. There is no shade that she cannot find and no shade that she cannot remove. I will take you to her."

"Talking of the sky, look, look at that beautiful rainbow," Kabbi gasped with excitement.

Robi twisted around to look. "The Great Painter in the Sky has done her job well. But wait a minute. What is happening to the rainbow? It is breaking up."

Even as they watched, the rainbow broke up into little moving dots. The dots formed a circle, then a figure eight, then a linked chain, then a big star, then the shape of an arrow. It was like looking into a kaleidoscope.

The dots were also getting closer and closer. Soon they were right above Robi and Kabbi. The dots were dancing.

"A-mazing, a-mazing," squeaked Kabbi, jumping in delight at the spectacle.

"It is not a rainbow at all!" exclaimed Robi. "These are butterflies."

Every single dot was a butterfly that moved with the grace ᵗ ɩcer. The butterflies worked so well as a team that pattern that they could not form. They could do ɦey could do tumbles and they could even spin on ɪngle wing.

Robi and Kabbi watched in wonder as the performance above their heads came to an end, and all the butterflies bent over to take a bow.

"A-mazing, a-mazing," squeaked Kabbi as he clapped.

Robi clapped too, but his clapping soon slowed down. He saw something that troubled him.

As the butterflies flew off, there was one that seemed unable to keep up with them. It fluttered in the air, dropped a little, fluttered some more, and then dropped to the ground.

It was a beautiful thing, all blue and purple and gold. It now lay helpless, weakly moving one wing.

"Oh dear, oh dear," Robi said. "We must do something."

"Oh yes, oh yes, oh yes," squeaked Kabbi, "we must."

Robi walked over to the butterfly, carrying Kabbi with him. They both peered down at the helpless creature.

"Miss Butterfly," Robi said, "I am so sorry to see you like this. Tell me, how may I assist you? I would really like to help."

"And I would like to help too," Kabbi added.

"I don't know what anybody can do," sobbed the butterfly. "You see, one of my wings is broken. All my friends have gone. I just cannot keep up with them anymore."

"Don't fret," Robi said, "I'm sure we can make you well again. Now, you shouldn't be lying on the cold, damp earth. Just come into my ear where it is safe and warm."

"Yes, yes. It is very cozy in there," agreed Kabbi. "I highly recommend it."

"Please come up my trunk," Robi offered. "Kabbi, Kabbi Wahabbi, my friend here, will help you, I'm sure. By the way, my name is Robi, Robi Dobi."

"And my name is Maya Wishkaya . . . of The Dancing

Butterflies. I come from The Land of the North Wind. Thank you so much for your kindness."

Kabbi crawled down Robi's trunk. "Climb onto my back," he said to Maya, "and I'll carry you up into Robi's ear. Can you manage to do that?"

"Oh, I am sure I can," said the grateful butterfly.

Slowly and carefully Kabbi carried her all the way up Robi's trunk and into his cozy ear.

"It is very comfortable here," Maya said as she slipped from Kabbi's back. The effort had exhausted her.

"Now you just lie down and rest and we will find something for you to eat, won't we, Robi! What would you like? What would you like to eat more than anything else?"

"We dancers like to eat lightly. Nectar, dusted with a little pollen, would be just perfect," said Maya, her eyes getting

rounder just thinking of this treat.

"Is nectar the same as honey?" Kabbi wanted to know.

"Not quite," Maya explained. "Nectar is what comes straight out of the flower. It is pure. It is delicious. The bees take nectar from the flowers and change it into honey. Honey is much thicker and sweeter. We prefer nectar because it is lighter. But please, I don't want you to go to any trouble looking for it."

Robi, of course, had heard all this and said, "It won't be any trouble. I know a wonderful spot, just where the forest ends. There are nut trees there and banana groves. The trees are covered with orchids of all shapes and sizes. Between the trees and a rushing stream is open land—the sweetest meadow you can ever hope to find. Wild larkspurs and lupines, double buttercups and primroses cover it like a carpet. We will go there and have a picnic."

And that is what they did. Robi put Maya on the tip of his trunk so all she had to do was lean forward to suck the nectar from the orchids that were high in the trees and from the buttercups that were low on the ground. Robi himself had a good helping of bananas and banana leaves while Kabbi ran around collecting nuts and seeds.

"If I wasn't orange, if I wasn't so far from home, if I wasn't worrying about my family, I would really enjoy this," Kabbi said.

"I *was* wondering why you are orange," Maya ventured, "but I did not like to ask."

So Kabbi told Maya his long story. She listened silently, batting her long eyelashes in sympathy.

Robi turned to Maya and added, "And that is why we are on our way to see The Great Painter in the Sky. She will surely know where to find the water that will wash off this paint. But tell us about you. How is it that you are so far from your home? How did you come to break your wing and how can we help you mend it?"

"It's a long story," Maya said.

"Tell us, tell us," Robi said. "We have all the time in the world. We won't set out to find The Great Painter in the Sky until early tomorrow morning."

"Well," Maya began, "I should perhaps begin with my very first memory," and she settled down to tell her story.

THREE

Maya Wishkaya's Story

"It was a cold, blustery morning. I remember a great stiffness in my body as I tried to come out of my cocoon. My wings felt stiff, my legs felt stiff, and my neck could barely turn. I poked my head out first and almost had to pull back because of the freezing wind. I was high up on a tree. It must have been springtime because there were young budding leaves on the branches.

"With great difficulty, I managed to push my wings out, but before I could open them properly, a current of wind swept me away. I tumbled over and over, and was carried very far from my home.

"I never knew my parents, or any member of my family. The wind had carried me to a distant part of my country and left me, half-dead, on top of a rock.

"I came out of my daze to the sound of 'and-a-*one*, two, three, four, *one*, two, three, four. . . .' I looked up and there, right above me, was a group of the most beautiful butterflies you could ever see. They were dancing.

"Perhaps I should say they were practicing dancing. I heard their teacher say, 'And now we will form a fan. It will open and it will close. We will do that four times. Then the fan will open and stay open. Then the open fan will dance, twisting and turning through the sky. The pattern on today's fan will be a dragon. So arrange yourselves as we've been practicing. Quick,

quick, no wasting time. You know our motto. We cannot wait. We cannot be late.'

"That, of course, was the voice of the very strict Madame Rascova. I would get to know her much better later. As I lay there and watched the fan open and close, I knew that all I wanted to do was dance. Dance like the butterflies above me.

"I must have said that aloud because all the butterflies suddenly stopped dancing to look down at me. I heard one say, 'Oh look, there is a young one who wants to join us.' Then I heard Madame Rascova say, 'If she wants to do that, she had better have some talent and she had better hurry. You know our motto. We cannot wait. We cannot be late. Hurry, hurry.'

"It wasn't easy for me. My wings seemed glued together. I tried separating them, very carefully. Then I tried flapping them. Yes, I could flap them. I found myself slowly lifting. I was flying.

"Madame Rascova called out again, 'Hurry, hurry. We cannot wait. We cannot be late.'

"I flew higher and higher. Soon I was with all the others. Everyone began to clap. Everyone except Madame Rascova. 'Let's see what you can do, first. Let us see you fly in a straight line, flapping your wings evenly up and down, up and down.'

"I flew straight for a while but then I felt my wings weakening and I took a dip. I pulled myself up again and flew straight, then I took another dip. My wings were not flapping evenly.

"'Tut, tut, tut,' said Madame Rascova. 'Not promising, not at all.'

"'But see, see what I can do. I can . . . I can . . . tumble,' I said. I remembered being hurtled through the air, tumbling with my wings still unopened. I tried to repeat that. It worked. Everyone laughed and clapped. Even Madame Rascova allowed herself a smile.

" 'Child,' she said. 'You may join us. You seem very determined and I like that. I like that very much. We will train you. Then it is up to you to stay in shape. If for some reason you cannot fly, we will just have to leave you behind. You see, our motto is: We cannot wait. We cannot be late. The show must go on.'

" 'I'll stay in shape,' I promised. And so I joined the group. We went to every part of the world, and wherever we danced, we heard nothing but clapping and cheering. Everyone said we were the best company they had ever seen. I got better and better at my work, until one day Madame Rascova called for me and said that she was going to make me one of her principal dancers. And that is when the trouble started."

"What trouble? What happened?" Kabbi wanted to know.

"And how did you break your wing?" Robi asked.

"I did not want to be *one* of the principal dancers. I wanted to be *the* principal dancer. The prima ballerina. I thought I deserved it. I thought I was the best." At this Maya broke into sobs.

"Oh, please," Robi said. "Don't cry. We will help you. Tell us what happened next."

"Madame Rascova had just taught all the nine principal dancers a new pattern with new steps and new formations for our wings. We were to fly in a straight row first and then shoot straight up like arrows, our wings half-open like an upside-down V. Then we were to close our wings and drop straight down to the exact place where we had been and then open our wings, all at the same time, and fly again. 'Do not shoot up more than ten feet,' Madame Rascova warned, 'or you might hurt yourself.'

"Well, I did what Madame Rascova asked at first. It was so

easy for me. But as I was the butterfly in the middle, with four butterflies on each side of me, I thought it might look prettier if I jumped higher than the others. And I would also show Madame Rascova how good I was. First I jumped twelve feet, then fifteen, then twenty. It was still easy. I always timed it so I dropped down to the row of flying butterflies at the same time as the other eight.

"I decided to try twenty-five feet. The jumping up was not hard at all. I felt so proud of myself. Then I started to drop. I started going down, faster and faster. When I reached the other butterflies, and the time came for me to open my wings, I found I could not do it. My wings clung to my sides and would not open. I kept dropping.

"Just when I thought I would most surely crash, my wings did open. But the force of the wind broke one of them. I managed to fly for a while but I knew I was lagging behind. The last thing I heard was Madame Rascova's voice saying, 'We cannot wait. We cannot be late. The show must go on.' Then I fell to the ground and you know the rest."

"A-mazing, a-mazing," said Kabbi.

Maya Wishkaya bowed her head as big tears rolled out of her eyes. Robi could not bear to watch anyone in pain. "Please don't cry," he said. "We'll find a way to mend your wing."

"That is almost impossible," Maya sobbed. "We need a very special flexible glue. Only one tree, a very tall tree, produces it. It is called The Tree With the Flexible Glue, and it grows on a small island right in the middle of a big, deep lake in the Southern Mountains."

"Do you know where that is?" Kabbi asked.

"I have flown over it many, many times but I do not think I could find it from the ground," Maya answered.

"Don't worry, we will find a way," Robi said. "But first things first. We must visit The Great Painter in the Sky and take care of Kabbi. You rest comfortably in my ear until then."

"I will look after you," Kabbi said to Maya, "and get you whatever you need. If I wasn't orange, if I wasn't so far from home, if I wasn't worrying about my family, I could really be happy here with you and Robi."

FOUR

The Green Parrot Army

So Robi, Kabbi, and Maya set out to find The Great Painter in the Sky. Robi walked all day and all night, while Kabbi and Maya rested in his ear. Early the next morning they stopped for breakfast in a shady mango grove.

"Let us all sit under this large tree," Robi suggested. "It's nice and cool."

Now, it just so happened that a whole army of green parrots came and settled in the branches of the same tree. They seemed very agitated and were talking at once, their red beaks opening and shutting with great speed.

"I think they went north," said one.

"You must be crazy. I saw them with my own eyes, running south," said another.

"Do you both have rocks for eyes? They went east. Definitely east," said a third.

"West. West. They went west. They went in the same direction as the wind. And the wind is blowing from east to west," said a fourth.

"Why don't we split up and look in all four directions. There are certainly enough of us," said a fifth.

"Poor Princess Tara," said a sixth. "She is so delicate and gentle. And she has never been away from home."

"The king and queen are in a state of shock," added a seventh.

Just then the parrot army noticed that it had an audience.

"Excuse us," said the general of the parrot army, "but Her Highness, Princess Tara, has been kidnapped from The Kingdom of the Contented Parrots. Have any of you seen her?"

"No, we have not," answered Robi. "By the way, I am Robi Dobi, this is Kabbi Wahabbi, and this is Maya Wishkaya. Who has kidnapped her?"

"And I am General Aman. Our princess has been kidnapped by The Wicked Purple Panthers," said General Aman. "They—well, they are from The Kingdom of the Sourpuss, so what can you expect? They like to destroy happiness, wherever they find it. They found it in our kingdom, in our Royal Family.

"You see, we all adored our princess from the day she was born. She was pretty, of course. The most beautiful parrot in the world, to tell the truth. Even as a newborn parrot, when she smiled, she could make the sun come out on the cloudiest day.

"As she got older, she grew kind and gentle. She wasn't in the least bit stuck-up. She would play hide-and-seek with our

children, make little wheat cakes for the elderly—she would pick all the wheat grain herself, you know—and sing the sweetest songs." General Aman broke off, lowering his head gloomily.

"Do not despair," said Robi. "If we all get together, I am sure we will be able to find the princess. But please go on with your story. What happened to the princess? How was she kidnapped?"

"Well, The Kingdom of the Sourpuss is just next door to ours," the General went on. "I think our happiness was too much for King Sourpuss and his court of The Wicked Purple Panthers. We used to watch them slinking by. They must have heard our songs and laughter. I think they were filled with envy. One day there was a knock on the palace door. I was standing just inside with several members of our army, so I opened the door. It turned out to be King Sourpuss himself with about fifty of his courtiers. They marched straight up to the king and queen, and without so much as a greeting, King Sourpuss said, 'I have come to marry your daughter.'

"Perhaps they wanted to take away our happiness. Perhaps they thought that our princess might teach them how to bring joy into their own lives. Who knows!

"Of course, our king could have just refused. But being the polite gentleman that he is, he said, 'We will leave it up to our daughter to decide these things. If you would kindly follow us into the garden where Princess Tara is spending the afternoon with her friends, you may ask her yourself.'

"The princess was in The Walled Mango Garden. We all trooped in there. Swings had been set up on the branches of many trees and the princess was swinging and singing with her friends.

"As soon as King Sourpuss spotted the princess, he yelled, 'Come here, Princess Tara.'

" 'Please, let her finish her song,' our king suggested gently.

"King Sourpuss only glared, and called out, 'Princess Tara, come with me. I want you to live in *my* court as *my* wife—as Queen Sourpuss.'

" 'I am terribly sorry,' Princess Tara replied politely, 'but I have no desire to leave my home just yet, or to marry until I meet the one that I can love. But thank you for asking me.'

"King Sourpuss bared his teeth, hissing, 'Willing or not, you are coming with me,' and he grabbed our princess and leapt over the garden wall. Some of his courtiers pushed back the startled king and queen, others held knives to our throats and before we knew it, The Wicked Purple Panthers had all jumped over the wall and disappeared.

"We flew after them but they were too fast for us. They live in The Big Brown Rocky Cave that is closed shut with a huge boulder, you know. If they are already home, there is no way we can get in to save the princess. The boulder works as a draw-bridge and once it is pulled shut, it can only be let down from the inside."

"How very sad. How heartbreaking," said Maya.

"A-mazing, a-mazing," said Kabbi.

"There must be something we can do," said Robi. "We cannot leave the princess in the hands of The Wicked Purple Panthers. We must organize a rescue. First of all, I must ask you, Kabbi, if you mind very much our delaying the search for The Great Painter in the Sky. . . . "

"No problem, no problem," squeaked Kabbi. "Please don't even think about it. Princess Tara needs our help, first and foremost."

"All right," said Robi, taking charge. "Let us all think. The Wicked Purple Panthers are probably heading home. Which direction is that?"

"South," offered General Aman.

"Let us go in that direction, then," Robi went on. "And let us keep a watchful eye so we do not miss anything. Kabbi, you'd better sit on the tip of my trunk, which I will keep low and close to the ground. From there you will be able to search the earth for clues. General Aman, if you and your army fly in close formation just ahead of me, you might be able to spot the panthers from a distance. Maya, you'd better tuck yourself into a safe corner in my ear. We will have to move fast and this may be a bumpy ride."

And so they set off toward the south.

FIVE

A Daring Rescue

They searched everywhere: in the bushes, along the rivers, and up steep hills. Just when they were all exhausted and thinking of resting for the night, Kabbi shouted out:

"A parrot feather! Could Princess Tara have a feather that is yellow with orange and red?"

"Yes, yes, yes," called out General Aman from the sky, "only she has those rare feathers."

Just then Robi said, "I see lots of eyes in the dark . . . eyes moving south on that hill. It must be them. Let us go as fast as we can. But let us be as quiet as we can."

So they moved on quickly, following the eyes that were loping ahead in the dark. Once they even heard the princess cry out. They could do nothing except follow. They were still very far behind.

"We're getting closer to The Big Brown Rocky Cave," General Aman whispered as he flew beside Robi's ear. "Once the panthers get inside, it will be impossible to save the princess."

They were moving quickly, but The Wicked Purple Panthers were even faster. They watched in horror as the boulder rolled open. The panthers raced inside and the boulder was drawn shut. Princess Tara was trapped.

By the time Robi and his friends reached The Big Brown

Rocky Cave, there was nothing to see but a little bit of light coming from a barred window high up on the cliff.

"The window has no ledge to perch on," said General Aman, "but I will fly past it and see what I see."

"And I will climb up to the bars and see what I can see," said Kabbi.

General Aman circled the window a few times.

"I cannot see her," he said. "I cannot see Her Highness, Princess Tara. I do see King Sourpuss though. And at least a hundred panthers. They seem to be muttering something."

Kabbi was still busy climbing, huffing and puffing as he went. When he got to the window, he discovered that the bars

were very close together. "I will try and squeeze in," he said to himself. He pulled in his breath, made himself very thin, and tried to squeeze through the bars. It did not work. He pulled in his breath even more. It still did not work. The third time he sucked in his breath so much that he became almost as flat as cardboard. Then he slipped in.

"Oh, oh, oh," cried Maya, who had now climbed to the edge of Robi's ear for a better view of the unfolding drama. "The panthers will surely kill Kabbi with a single swipe of their claws."

"Please do not worry," said Robi. "Kabbi is very clever."

Kabbi was clever. Slowly he crept down the wall on the inside. Flushed with success, The Wicked Purple Panthers were too busy chanting to notice him, though whenever one of them turned in his direction he wisely froze to the spot.

Kabbi saw that Princess Tara was in a large cage hanging from the ceiling of the cave. The panthers were all around her. He crept down to the floor and made his way to the boulder entrance. It was the only way to get in or out. He noticed that the boulder was held in place by two thick ropes. It would take at least fifty panthers to lower it and pull it up.

Just then he heard King Sourpuss say, "Bring the priest to me. Let the ceremony begin. My bride and I will walk around the sacred flame seven times. Once the seventh round is completed, it will mean that we are married. We will be forever King and Queen Sourpuss."

"I won't walk around the fire with you," cried Princess Tara. "Please let me go home. My parents will be very worried."

"Let them worry for the rest of their lives! You will never leave this cave. Never, never, never. Now you are mine," sneered King Sourpuss. "If you will not willingly walk with me, I will just have to carry you around the flame in your cage. We will be married one way or another."

"Oh dear," muttered Kabbi, "we must do something fast."

He scampered up the wall to the barred window again, breathed in to push himself through the bars, and then jumped down onto Robi's back.

"I am so happy you are safe," declared Maya.

"We have to hurry. They are about to be married. The princess is in a cage and the boulder is held up by two thick ropes," Kabbi said breathlessly.

Robi thought quickly. "I have a plan," he announced. "Our brave Kabbi will just have to go back and bite through some of the ropes. I will hold the boulder in place with my back until we are ready. The princess should be warned that a rescue is going on or she may be frightened. We must find a sign to let her know that her friends are here. A sign . . . a sign . . . What could we use for a sign?"

"How about one of my smaller feathers? The princess will recognize the green feathers of her father's army," offered General Aman, pulling out one of his feathers with his beak.

"Good, very good. Let us start right away, Kabbi. Give us two long whistles when you are ready," Robi said.

Again Kabbi climbed up to the small window, this time carrying a small green feather in his mouth, and pushed himself through the bars. Once inside he climbed straight up to the ceiling, and crawled upside down until he reached the rod that held the cage.

This was the tricky part. He had to get down the rod without being seen by any of the panthers.

Luckily they did not look toward the cage, but when he was halfway down, Princess Tara looked up and saw a terrifying orange creature above her. She had just opened her beak to scream, when

Kabbi dropped the green feather into her cage. Kabbi knew that Princess Tara understood immediately, because she opened up her wings and hid him from the view of the panthers.

But Kabbi had another important task to perform. The door of the cage still had to be opened. To do this he would have to pull up the long pin that held it closed, but the door would, of course, have to appear to be shut so as not to give the rescue operation away. This task was particularly dangerous, as the panthers could spot him from below.

The panthers, however, were still busy chanting. The priest had gathered small offerings of dead crows and arranged them in bowls around the sacred flame. King Sourpuss called out, "Where is my wedding crown? Will someone get me my wedding crown?"

Kabbi knew he had to hurry. He managed to pull up the

pin, but it kept slipping down again. With nothing else at hand, he bit off one of his whiskers and used it to tie the pin to the cage, so that it was held open. He made sure the door appeared shut, and scrambled up the rod again, across the ceiling, down the wall, and along the floor to the boulder.

Then he began gnawing at the ropes. It was hard going because they were very thick.

The wedding ceremony had begun. The priest began by chanting:

"Willibub, willibub, willibub,
King Sourpuss,
All angry, all discontented, and all mean,
Now starteth the Seven Circles of Matrimony
With Princess Tara,
Willibub, willibub, willibub."

"You may now begin the first circle," he added, throwing some oil into the flame so that it flared up.

"Are you going to walk with me," asked King Sourpuss, "or will I have to resort to stronger means?"

"I could never walk with you around this flame, or anywhere else for that matter. I do not love you. Please let me go home," Princess Tara pleaded, as politely and reasonably as ever.

King Sourpuss angrily pulled the cage off its hook.

The door of the cage started to swing open but the princess quickly held it shut with her claws.

Holding the cage up with his paw, King Sourpuss began the first circle.

Oh my, oh my, thought Kabbi to himself, I'd better hurry up. He kept gnawing on the rope.

Outside the cave, Robi was leaning hard on the boulder. He did not want it to roll open before all preparations were complete. Maya was still hanging on to the edge of his ear, worrying about Kabbi, while General Aman and his army of green parrots were zooming past the window, relaying the latest information.

"The wedding has started," said one parrot.

"Kabbi is still biting on the first rope," said a second parrot.

"The door of the cage is on system 'Go,'" reported the general.

Kabbi finished gnawing through the first rope and started nibbling furiously on the second. His jaw was aching badly, but he couldn't stop now.

King Sourpuss peered into the cage, saying, "And now there are only two more rounds to go before you are mine."

The priest was chanting:

"Willibub, willibub, willibub,
King Sourpuss,
All angry, all discontented, and all mean,
Now starteth the Sixth Circle of Matrimony
With Princess Tara,
Willibub, willibub, willibub."

Oh my, oh my, thought Kabbi to himself, I had better hurry.

Just as the seventh and final circle began, he bit through the last strand of the rope. Robi now had the full weight of the boulder against his shoulder. He heard Kabbi's two long whistles. "Are we ready?" asked Robi. "One, two, and . . ."

With that, Robi pushed the boulder to one side. Everyone rushed inside at the same time. General Aman and all the parrots

flew around and around, squawking loudly and causing
confusion. Robi, with Maya still dangling from his ear, trumpeted over and over again, and then, when he was near the
cage, whispered, "Onto my back, Princess Tara, quick, quick!"

Princess Tara pushed open the door of the cage and in one swift movement rushed past Maya and onto Robi's back.

"Kabbi, Kabbi, where are you, Kabbi?" called Maya.

Robi realized that it was time to get out. The panthers were beginning to attack. Where was Kabbi?

"I'm here, I'm here," squeaked Kabbi, running up Robi's tail. Soon he had joined Maya inside the welcoming ear.

Robi trumpeted once more and charged out. The parrots left with him, flying above him, beside him, and even between his legs. The panthers started to follow, but before they could get out, Robi pushed the boulder back into place.

The Big Brown Rocky Cave was now shut. With no ropes to lower their boulder entrance, The Wicked Purple Panthers and King Sourpuss would not be able to get out!

"We should all escort Princess Tara home," Robi suggested triumphantly.

"I would like to invite you all to my parents' palace," declared the princess, now flying along beside Robi's ear. "You can rest there, then feast with us before you go on your way."

"What a perfect idea," said Maya. "My nerves are on edge."

"Just an a-mazing adventure, an a-mazing adventure," said Kabbi, who was sitting near the princess and Maya. "If I wasn't orange, if I wasn't so far from home, if I wasn't worrying about my family, I would really enjoy this."

"Oh please," said Princess Tara, "tell me how you both came to be here. Why you are so orange and why do you have a broken wing?"

So Kabbi and Maya both told their stories to Princess Tara. By the time they had finished, her eyes were full of warmth.

"I know the tree you speak about,'" said the princess to Maya. "The one that has the flexible glue bubbling from the inside of its trunk. It is in our kingdom. I have seen it many times."

"You have, you have?" asked Kabbi, now very excited. "You know where it is?"

"You know where it is?" repeated Robi, who of course could hear everything, since the conversation was going on in his ear.

"I could easily guide you there," offered Princess Tara, "but do not get your hopes up. The Tree With the Flexible Glue you speak of grows on a small island right in the middle of a deep lake in the Southern Mountains. The glue is to be found inside its narrow, hollow trunk. It oozes from its very core and must be used fresh, while it is still warm and soft. It hardens in less than a minute. The only way to enter the hollow trunk is from the top, and the inside walls are very slippery. If anyone tries to crawl inside, they lose their footing, fall into the glue, and disappear in seconds."

"Do not worry, Maya Wishkaya," Robi said. "We will find a way. Kabbi, I know we planned to take care of your orange appearance first, but since The Tree With the Flexible Glue is right here in The Kingdom of the Contented Parrots . . . "

"Oh, please, please," said Kabbi, "I understand perfectly. Let us take care of Maya first. And if there is anything I can do to help . . ."

"Then it is settled," said Princess Tara. "First we will go to the palace to rest. Then, in the morning I will guide you to The Tree With the Flexible Glue. But now, tell me what you would like to eat most of all so that I can send General Aman and the army ahead of us with your requests."

"We would be happy with anything . . . " Robi started to say.

"But we would like to offer you what you would enjoy the most," Princess Tara said.

"In that case," said Kabbi, "how about some freshly roasted peanuts for me?"

"Perhaps some nectar lightly dusted with pollen for me," suggested Maya.

"Oh well, in that case, some bunches of bananas and a few lumps of raw sugar for me," said Robi.

General Aman and his army flew off with all the special requests. By the time Robi and his friends arrived at the palace, the entire Kingdom of the Contented Parrots was waiting for them with banners and flags, cheering and clapping.

They spent the rest of the night feasting and resting.

SIX

The Tree With the Flexible Glue

Early the next morning it was time to set out again. Princess Tara flew overhead, directing Robi to The Tree With the Flexible Glue. Kabbi kept Maya company in Robi's ear. When they got to the lake, Robi realized at once that this was going to be an extremely difficult task. The lake was deep and the tree was very tall.

He began to think. "I have a plan," he said to his friends.

"You have, have you?" said Kabbi. "A-mazing, a-mazing."

"I will need your help, Kabbi," Robi said.

"Anytime," Kabbi answered.

"I need to get closer to the top of the tree," said Robi. "For that, I need to stand on something very high. Something like a . . . a . . . hill. What about *that* one?"

Robi pointed to a hill not too far from them.

"How can we carry a hill across a lake?" Kabbi asked.

"I will have to balance it on the tip of my trunk," Robi explained. "We also need a long pole. We should be able to find one in this bamboo forest."

Robi pulled up the longest bamboo he could find and wrapped his trunk firmly around it. Then he nudged the whole hill with his forehead until it detached itself from the ground. He lifted the hill and balanced it very carefully on the tip of his trunk.

"Are we all ready?" he called out to his friends. "Let's go. Maya and Robi, you stay in my ear. I am going to start swimming across the lake."

And so Robi, with a whole hill balanced on the tip of his trunk, slowly, carefully stepped into the deep lake and began swimming to the island in the middle.

With the hill in front of his eyes, it was hard for Robi to see where he was going, but Princess Tara directed him from above. "A little to the right . . . now a little to the left . . . "

As Robi swam, water drifted into his ears.

"Let's move higher up," gasped Kabbi, helping Maya to an upper corner in the ear. "You will not get wet here."

"Don't move too much inside, or I will drop the hill," Robi warned.

"You are now at the island," Princess Tara called out. "The tree is on your left."

Robi carried the hill right up to the tree and put it down. Then, with his trunk still wrapped around the pole, he climbed up to the top of the hill. From here he could look down the hollow tree trunk. The walls of the trunk were smooth and slippery, just as Princess Tara had described. At the bottom he could see the bubbling red-hot glue.

"All right, brave Kabbi, it is up to you now," Robi said. "Maya, you should climb on to Kabbi's back. He will take you inside the tree. I will hold the long pole with the tip of my trunk and hang it inside the hollow tree. First you will both go down my trunk and then down the pole until you reach the glue. But be careful—the glue is very hot. Kabbi, you should carry a twig in your mouth. It will be up to you to collect a little glue on the twig and quickly apply it to Maya's wing. Then hurry back up as fast as you can."

"I will get you a twig," Princess Tara offered, and she flew to a bush to find one of the right size.

Kabbi put the twig in his mouth. Then Maya climbed onto his back. The two then began the slow descent, first down Robi's trunk and then down the pole. They could see the fiery glue bubbling below. Kabbi and Maya knew that one false step would be the end of them.

"My feet are slipping," screamed Kabbi.

He was holding on to the pole but sliding fast, fast, fast . . . Maya was clinging to him for dear life.

Just as he got close to the glue, Kabbi managed to stop himself by holding onto a bump in the pole.

Bubble, bubble, bubble. The thick glue rose out of the very heart of the tree.

"The heat . . . the heat is unbearable," murmured Maya.

Kabbi lowered the twig. He could not reach the glue.

He slid down to the very tip of the pole and lowered the twig. He still could not reach the glue.

"Hold on tight," he said to Maya.

Kabbi clung to the tip of the pole with one paw and lowered the rest of his body over the glue.

"Please don't take such a risk. Let's just forget my wing. I do not have to fly again. Let's just go back up, where we can feel the wind and see the sky," Maya pleaded.

Kabbi was now hanging on to the pole with just one little claw. He lowered the twig one more time.

"I've got it," he cried. "I have got a drop of glue. Quick, Maya, let me put it on your wing."

Kabbi pulled himself back up onto the pole and when he was steady he applied the glue to Maya's wing with the tip of the twig.

"It is hot. It stings," Maya cried.

But within seconds the glue had cooled and Maya's wing was whole again. She moved it up and down. It worked!

Together they slowly crept up the pole and then up Robi's trunk. They kept going until they reached the top of the elephant's head, and then everyone shouted together, "We did it, we did it!"

Maya began to flutter her wings and then she took off, doing loops and circles in the sky. "I can fly again," she cried.

Kabbi looked a little sad. "Are you going to leave us now?"

"We still have to go to Kamala-Saurus, The Great Painter in the Sky, don't we?" Maya asked. "We still have to find a way to wash that orange stuff off. Can we not stay together until Kabbi is normal again?"

And so it was decided that Princess Tara and Maya Wishkaya would join Robi and Kabbi on their search for Kamala-Saurus.

First Robi had to return the hill to its original position. He slowly swam back, carrying it across the lake on the tip of his trunk.

"A-mazing, a-mazing," said Kabbi, sprawled out on the side of the hill. "If I wasn't orange, if I wasn't so far from home, if I wasn't worrying about my family, I would really enjoy this."

"We have to head north," said Robi. "I know Kamala-Saurus lives in the mountains—the tallest mountains in the world. This makes it easier for her to reach the sky. It will be cold and snowy up there."

"I am used to the cold," Maya said.

"And I will manage just fine," said Princess Tara.

"Of course, if anyone feels chilly they can come into my ear to get warm. It is always cozy in there," said Robi.

They set off for the north. Maya and the princess acted as scouts, going ahead to check out the land and to see what lay in the distance. Kabbi often sat up on Robi's back.

They journeyed this way for many days, finding sheltered places to sleep at night.

The mountains got higher and higher, the air colder and colder.

One day as the group was crossing a mountain stream and snow was falling all around them, Princess Tara peeped out of Robi's ear and then flew off on a scouting trip. "I think I can see something in the distance. On top of that mountain. I can see what looks like a long neck . . . with a small head . . . and holding a brush," she said.

Robi looked toward the horizon, through the haze of snow. Yes, it did appear to be Kamala-Saurus, on top of the highest mountain.

With his friends tucked in his ear for safety and warmth, Robi trudged through thick snow as fast as he could go in the direction of the distant mountain.

With every step he found himself sinking deeper into the snow. Soon Robi could barely move, but he kept pushing the snow away with his trunk and tail. Maya, Kabbi, and Tara were busy clearing snow out of his ear.

"A-mazing, a-mazing," said Kabbi, who had never seen snow before.

"How far are we from The Great Painter in the Sky?" Maya asked.

"We have one more mountain to climb," said Robi, "but it

is the most difficult one yet. Kabbi, bring out the rope that is coiled in the back of my ear."

In front of them was a sheer cliff.

Kabbi dragged out the rope and laid it on Robi's back.

"Princess Tara and Maya, I will need your assistance as well," Robi said. "If you could take the end of the rope and tie it tightly to that long stone that is jutting out on top of the cliff, it would be a great help. I am going to pull myself up."

Princess Tara and Maya flew up with the rope and tied it to the stone with several strong knots. Then they both waited for Robi.

Kabbi decided to crawl up next to Robi, giving him all the helpful advice he could.

Using his front legs to haul himself up and his back legs to steady himself on the rope, Robi began his climb.

"You can rest your back feet on this ledge, right here," Kabbi suggested.

Robi was breathing heavily, but slowly and steadily he was inching up.

"It is not much farther," encouraged Princess Tara and Maya. "You are almost there."

It had stopped snowing by the time Robi and Kabbi reached the top. It was also getting dark.

They rested on top of the cliff for the night.

SEVEN

The Great Painter in the Sky

It was just beginning to get light when they awoke. What greeted them was the most beautiful sight they had ever seen. There was Kamala-Saurus, right above them, painting the dawn. With a brush held in her mouth, she was filling the sky with great splashes of purple and red.

"A-mazing, a-mazing," cried Kabbi.

Princess Tara burst into song and Maya did a few twirls in the air.

"We are almost there, dear Kabbi," Robi said. "Now you can become yourself again."

Kamala-Saurus was surprised to see them. "And who is this troop of strangers?" she asked in her ancient voice. "Almost no one visits me here. And how pretty you both are," she went on as she studied both Princess Tara and Maya. "I love your yellow," she said to the princess, "and I love your blue," she said to Maya. "I think I will put both in the sky today!"

She bent her long neck to mix some more hues and began painting parrot yellow and butterfly blue into the dawn.

Then she spotted Kabbi. "Now that is a strange-looking mouse . . ." she began. But when she saw Kabbi's lip quiver with unhappiness, she stopped. "Oh dear, have I said the wrong thing?"

"Oh no, no . . ." Kabbi replied hastily.

"That is why we are here," explained Robi. "It's a long story."

"I have plenty of time," Kamala-Saurus said. "Come, sit near me while I paint and tell me what happened."

So they all sat down and told her about their adventures and how Kabbi came to be an orange mouse.

"We know that you are the only person with the special waters that can wash this permanent paint away," Robi added.

"Well, you are right in one way, and wrong in another," said Kamala-Saurus. "I know where such waters exist, but I do not have them with me here."

Kabbi looked terribly disappointed.

Robi immediately said, "But where can these waters be found? We will go anywhere to get them."

"We will indeed," said Maya. "We will stay with Kabbi until he turns back to his natural brown."

"We will indeed," added Princess Tara.

"I cannot leave my place here at the top of the mountain," Kamala-Saurus said, "but I can give you detailed instructions to get to The Cave of Healing Liquids. If you follow them very carefully, there is no reason why you cannot find the waters and make a bath that will wash off the paint."

"Just tell us the way," Robi said. "I have a good memory and will remember everything you say."

"All right then, listen carefully," Kamala-Saurus began. "First you go down this mountain, not the way you came but the other way. It is much easier. When you get to the bottom, turn west. Walk straight ahead until you come to The Three Sister Rocks. You will recognize them because they look alike and are near each other. Turn left and walk exactly one hundred paces. You will see a cave. This is The Cave of Healing Liquids. Enter the cave. There will be steps leading down, down, down. Keep following them. When you reach the bottom, you will find a room in which there are several pools of water.

"The water in each pool is slightly different. I will give you three shade cards. The three types of water you need match the shades on the cards exactly."

Kamala-Saurus pulled out three cards and brushed one with a shade of aqua, another with a shade of green, and a third with a shade of deep blue. She also gave them a bowl and a cup.

"Match the shades carefully and take exactly one cup of water from each pond, then put each one into the bowl. There is also a small waterfall in the cave that drips white liquid—one drop every minute. Hold the bowl under this waterfall and collect just one drop. That is all you need. This is the mixture that will wash off Kabbi's permanent paint."

As Robi and his friends started their descent, Kamala-Saurus said, "Here, take this toboggan. The easiest way down is to slide."

So Robi sat on the toboggan and Kabbi, Maya, and Princess Tara settled themselves on his curled-up trunk.

And down they went.

Wheeeeeee.

Before they knew it, they were at the bottom of the mountain.

"A-mazing, a-mazing," said Kabbi. "If I wasn't orange, if I wasn't so far from home, if I wasn't worrying about my family, I would really enjoy this."

"You won't be orange for long," said Robi, who was already leading them west. "I think I spot The Three Sister Rocks."

When they got to the rocks, Robi said, "And now we turn left and walk a hundred paces."

They started counting, "One, two, three . . .

"ninety-eight, ninety-nine, one hundred."

"This must be The Cave of Healing Liquids," Robi said.

They were in the mouth of a cave. It looked dark inside. But once they went in they found that little circles of light were coming in from many different sources, from little openings in the cave that they could hardly see.

They started going down the winding steps. Here, too, little dots of dancing light brightened their way. Soon they found themselves in a magical room. They could hear water making many different sounds—waves splashing, drops dripping, brooks bubbling—all forming a beautiful symphony.

They listened, entranced.

"We should look for the pools," said Robi.

There were pools all around them, at different levels, some small and some big, each holding a different shade of water.

Robi pulled out the shade cards from his ear. "Now let us all try and match them. Maya, you take one card. Princess Tara, you take another, and Kabbi, you take the third. I will hold the basin and cup with my trunk."

Maya fluttered to one pond, and said, "This shade is almost right, but it isn't quite the blue I need."

"And this one," said Princess Tara, "is not quite the right green."

"I think I have found the aqua," cried Kabbi.

"Here, take the cup, fill it, and pour the water into this basin," Robi said.

Kabbi did as he was told.

"I have matched my blue," Maya called out. "May I please have the cup?" She fetched her water and poured it into the basin as well.

"And I have finally found my green shade," said Princess Tara, pouring her water in. "Now we have all we need."

"Except the one drop of white," Robi added. "Where is the little waterfall?"

They looked around the cave. They could not see it.

Robi had an idea.

"Listen carefully to the water's music," he suggested. "When you hear the sound of a drop of water, try to guess where it came from. Let's all listen carefully."

They were silent and listened to the music of the waters. Just after the sound of crashing waves there was a pause. . . . There it was, the sound of a drop of water, falling. Yes. They all looked up. The sound was coming from the top of the cave.

Immediately Maya flew high up and looked around. "Yes," she called down. "It is up here, a tiny waterfall with white water."

"Give us the basin," said Maya and Princess Tara to Robi. "We will fly to the top of the cave and collect the white drop that we need."

Holding the basin between them, they flew up and held it beneath the waterfall. Soon a little white water droplet began to form. It dropped into the basin.

Maya and Princess Tara flew down with it and put it on the floor of the cave.

"This is it, Kabbi," declared Robi.

Kabbi climbed up onto the edge of the basin. He balanced on the edge for a while, looking this way and that.

"Dear, oh dear," he said. "This is a momentous occasion," and with that, he slid in.

His friends watched him disappear under the water. They held their breath.

Where was Kabbi?

A little head poked out of the water. It was brown. A little more of the body came out. It was brown too. Kabbi leapt out of the water. "I am brown again!" he cried.

"He is brown again," Robi, Maya, and Princess Tara said in chorus.

"A-mazing, a-mazing," said Kabbi. "If I wasn't so far from home, if I wasn't worrying about my family, I would really be so happy."

"Most of us have to head south anyway," Robi said. "Princess Tara does, and so do I. Why don't we take you home and see if we can find your family?"

"Oh, would you do that, would you really do that?" asked Kabbi. "And what about you, Maya? Is it time to say good-bye?"

"Absolutely not," Maya replied. "The Dancing Butterflies are going to perform in the south over a small pond not far from Trig-nig-wig-put-num. I could join them after we have all taken Kabbi home. Let's stay together until then."

"Oh yes," said Princess Tara.

"Why not?" said Robi.

"A-mazing, a-mazing," said Kabbi.

EIGHT

Another Brave Rescue

So Robi and his friends took off for the south. First they passed forests of rhododendrons, then fields of wheat, then groves of oranges. When they began to see palm trees and rice paddies, they knew they were close.

Kabbi climbed up on top of Robi's head and looked around. "My home—what used to be my home—is just a short distance away. But my family, my poor family . . . I do not know what has happened to them. The only one who knows is Slimy Kimey the snake-witch. We have to find her."

"I have a plan," offered Robi. "You all stay in my ear for the time being. Slimy Kimey will not attack me easily."

Robi then walked up to a palm tree and asked, "Can you tell me where Slimy Kimey the snake-witch lives?"

"You mean the one with the bad breath, the one that snatches up all the mice?" the palm tree said. "She lives in that red house at the end of the lane with all the lights shining and smoke coming out of the chimney. Slimy Kimey must be cooking. She cooks all night."

Robi walked up to the red house and knocked on the door.

"Who is it? Who is it?" screeched the snake-witch. "I am busy."

Robi knocked again.

"'Who is it? Who is it?" screeched the snake-witch again. "Go away, I am busy cooking."

"I am Robi Dobi the elephant, looking for some food and shelter for the night," Robi said.

"Go away, go away," said the snake-witch. "All my food is for me. And nobody is invited to my house. I never share. Go away."

Maya had heard all this and whispered, "I will fly in through the chimney and see what is going on inside."

"But there is smoke coming out of there. It will be hot and dangerous. Of course, if you breathe through a dampened piece of grass it will keep some of the smoke out," Kabbi said as he licked a soft blade of grass and tied it around Maya's mouth and nose.

"I will be very careful," said Maya, and she flew out of Robi's ear and toward the chimney. The others watched her hover above the chimney for a minute and then disappear inside.

The smoke was curling up through the middle of the chimney so Maya flew slowly down one corner, coughing and spluttering as she went. The wet grass helped. Down below was a blazing fire with a bubbling pot of water on top of it, but Maya avoided both the fire and steam by staying close to one side of the chimney.

Slimy Kimey was too busy chopping carrots and leeks to notice Maya. Various cookbooks were scattered on her worktable and she consulted them from time to time.

Maya looked around for the captured mice. Where were they? Were they already dead?

Then she heard some mouselike squeaks. She looked at the far wall of the kitchen. It was lined, from floor to ceiling, with clear plastic boxes, each with a few tiny holes for air. In every box was a family of mice and, of course, some rice for them to eat so they would get fat.

Maya fluttered up and down the rows of boxes. "The Wahabbi family? I am looking for the Wahabbi family. Are they still here?" she asked.

The mice, who were all orange, looked so sad. They pointed to a box near the floor. Maya fluttered over to it. "The Wahabbis?" she asked.

Father Wahabbi looked up in surprise. "Who are you, and how do you know our name?" he asked.

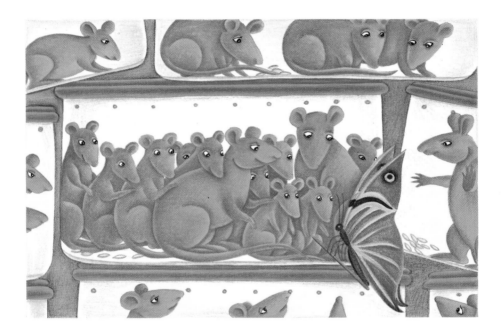

"I am a friend of your son Kabbi . . . " Maya began.

"Oh, poor Kabbi," cried Mother Wahabbi. "We do not know what has happened to him. The rest of the family is all here, but poor Kabbi was left at home with no food. He must have starved."

"Poor, poor Kabbi," said the Wahabbi brothers and sisters.

"Kabbi is just fine," said Maya. "In fact, he is outside with the rest of our friends. We have come to rescue you."

"Hide, hide," said Father Wahabbi to Maya. "Slimy Kimey is coming toward us."

Maya hid behind a box.

Slimy Kimey came toward the wall of mice, singing:

"I'm going to boil the rascals up
Then sauté them with carrots and leeks
Add almonds and raisins and apples and rum
And marinate them for several weeks."

She looked up and down the rows of boxes. "And who shall it be today? Who looks fat and juicy? Hmmm?"

She looked along one row, then along another, then another. Her eyes rested on the Wahabbis. "That family looks good enough to eat," she muttered.

Slimy Kimey pulled their box out and carried it to her worktable.

"We'd better hurry," said Maya to herself as she rushed over to the chimney. She flew out, the wet grass still protecting her, and hurtled toward Robi.

"We must hurry. The Wahabbis are in great danger," Maya cried.

"I have a plan," Robi said. "Quickly, get into my ear. I will deal with Slimy Kimey." And as he spoke, Robi crashed through the door with his head and charged into the house.

"Get out of my house," screeched Slimy Kimey. "You have got some nerve coming in here!" By this time Maya and Princess Tara had flown out of Robi's ear and were flying in circles around Slimy Kimey's head.

"All of you, get out, get out!" she yelled as she swung at Maya and Princess Tara with her rolling pin.

Just then Robi coiled his trunk around Slimy Kimey and picked her up.

"Let me down! Let me down or I will bite you and poison you," Slimy Kimey hissed.

But before she could do any such thing, Robi had dropped her into the pot of boiling water.

Slimy Kimey tried to jump out, but Robi quickly covered the pot with a heavy lid.

Kabbi rushed out of Robi's ear and ran to his family.

"Oh Kabbi," cried Mother Wahabbi, "you are all right."

Maya and Princess Tara flew around opening up all the plastic boxes. Soon hundreds of orange mice were running around the kitchen, singing, "We are free, we are free."

"And thanks to Robi, my friend here, I can even take you to a special, secret place to wash off the orange paint," Kabbi said.

"Let's go, let's go now," the mice chanted.

Everyone ran out of Slimy Kimey's red smoky house.

"A-mazing, a-mazing," said Kabbi, "I am not orange any-more, I am back home, I am not worrying about my family, and I am really enjoying myself."

"Why don't we celebrate by going to the small pond near-by, where The Dancing Butterflies appear," Robi suggested. "We will watch the performance together, and then say our good-byes. Tara has to go back to her parents in The Kingdom of the Contented Parrots.

"Maya will join The Dancing Butterflies, and I know that Kabbi wants to lead all the orange mice to The Cave of Healing Liquids. He knows the way. As for me, I must head home as well. But first, let us go and enjoy the dance performance together."

And that is what they did. With Kabbi sitting on Robi's head, Princess Tara and Maya led the way to the pond in the nearby village.

Sure enough, The Dancing Butterflies came flying in from the distant horizon and Maya flew up to join them. They danced and danced and danced, with Maya threading her way between formations of flowers and rings and triangles. When the group left, Maya was the last, waving until she could be seen no more.

"A-mazing, a-mazing," said Kabbi. "I will miss her. But I am sure she will come touring this way every year."

Princess Tara took off for her palace.

"You are welcome to come and stay with us, whenever you are passing through," she said, giving Robi a kiss on the tip of his trunk, and Kabbi a big hug with her wings. Then she flew off too.

Kabbi turned to the orange mice. "I will take you to The Cave of Healing Liquids," he said. "It will be a long and wonderful journey." And with a tearful thanks to Robi, he marched forward, an army of mice following behind.

Robi was left alone. He turned up his trunk, trumpeted good-bye to his friends, and began walking home. How good it will be to see my family again, he thought to himself, and to tell them about my many wonderful adventures.